Date Due

BRODART, CO.   Cat. No. 23-233-003   Printed in U.S.A.

Post Card Passages

written by Susan Joyce

illustrated by Doug DuBosque

PEEL
PRODUCTIONS

For Gladys —S.J.

For Hazie —D.D.

By the time young Suellan Weaver was learning to ride a tricycle, Great-Aunt Gladys had already traveled across North America many times and around the world once. A large, black leather bag was her constant companion. She kept the important things in it: her passport, wallet, traveler's checks, tickets, itinerary, address book, a notebook, two pens, a good book to read, binoculars, a handkerchief, a comb, a scarf and a small cosmetic pouch—with the overnight essentials, in case her checked luggage got lost.

Great-Aunt Gladys loved to share her travel adventures with family and friends by sending them picture post cards from the faraway places she visited. And so, the Weaver Family of Tucson, Arizona received many colorful post cards from all over the world...

69:—BRIDGING THE GOLDEN GATE, SAN FRANCISCO, CALIFORNIA

The Golden Gate Bridge from San Francisco to Marin County is the World's largest single span bridge. The main structure is 8,940 feet long. The towers above water are 746 feet high. The main span is 4200 feet long. There are two ten-foot sidewalks and six lanes for vehicular traffic, total width 90 feet. Total length including approaches is seven miles. Cost $35,000,000.

Weygant Card Distrs, San Francisco, Calif.

POST CARD

Remember - Only you can PREVENT FOREST FIRES

UNITED STATES
1 CENT 1

SAN FRANCISCO, CALIF.
OCT 2
8-PM
1952

Dear Hearts:

I'm enjoying visiting an old school friend this week. Tomorrow we will drive north along the scenic coast highway. I fondly remember your visit to Oklahoma last Christmas— seems like just days ago!

Love,

Aunt Glad

The Weaver Family
6068 E. Pima Street
Tucson, Arizona

ADDRESS

49257

THE PLAZA · NEW YORK

April 7, 1953

THE PLAZA

PLAZA CIRCLE at 59th ST., NEW YORK 19, N.Y.
*Ideally located where fashionable 5th Avenue meets
beautiful Central Park, The Plaza is close to all important social and
business activities.* HOME OF THE PERSIAN ROOM AND RENDEZ-VOUS.

Dear Hearts:

    My room at the Plaza has a
spectacular view of Central Park
and the city. I enjoyed lovely lilies in
Bermuda last week. I'm on my way
to Washington, D.C. tomorrow—
just in time to see the cherry
blossoms. Then I'm going home to
Oklahoma by train.

        Love, *Aunt Glad*

P.S. Happy 8th Birthday Suellen!

A HILTON HOTEL

AIR MAIL 6¢

NEW YORK
APR 7
2 30 PM
1953

"Air Mail"

HIRE THE HANDICAPPED

POST CARD

The Weaver Family

6068 E. Pima Street

Tucson, Arizona

April 15, 1953

Dear Diary:

Today we received another post card from Great-Aunt Gladys—and she wished me Happy Birthday! This one is of the Plaza Hotel in New York City. It's so-o-o beautiful! I wish I could go there. Mom says it takes *lots* of money to travel. I guess Aunt Gladys has lots of money. She stays in fancy hotels…I'm glad she sends us post cards and souvenirs from her travels. Sometimes I tie the luggage tags to Mom's old purses and pretend I'm Aunt Gladys…off to see the world. I'm going to send Aunt Gladys a post card from Tucson. One just from me. I'll send her a *really* beautiful one of the desert and ask her to write back and to address it to me, just *me*. I'm crossing my fingers and toes and hoping she will. Gotta go, it's lights out. Good night!

Love, *Suellan*

THIS SPACE FOR WRITING MESSAGES

Dear Aunt Gladys:

How are you? I am fine. So is my dog, Brownie. Do you like this picture of the desert? Thank you for sending us post cards and souvenirs. I save them in a special box. I like the pictures and the colorful stamps from other places. Could you please send a post card just to me. I would like to have one with my name on it. Gotta go now. Please write back. Love,

Suellan

TUCSON
MAY 16
9³⁰ M
2 · 1953
ARIZ

POST CARD

NEW HOPE FOR HEA
— SUPPORT —
THE HEART FU

Mrs. Gladys Haynes Frazier
1633 Camden Way,
Oklahoma City, Oklahoma

July 1954

Dear Suellan:

I'm in England this week with a group of friends from Oklahoma City. It's fun being here again and revisiting my favorite places—Piccadilly, Buckingham Palace, Westminster Abbey, St Paul's Cathedral, London Bridge & other historic sights. I enjoyed scones at tea this afternoon. Tonight we will attend the theatre. Lovely to hear from you. You can always write me at my Oklahoma City address. My mail gets forwarded when I'm traveling.

Love, *Aunt Glad*

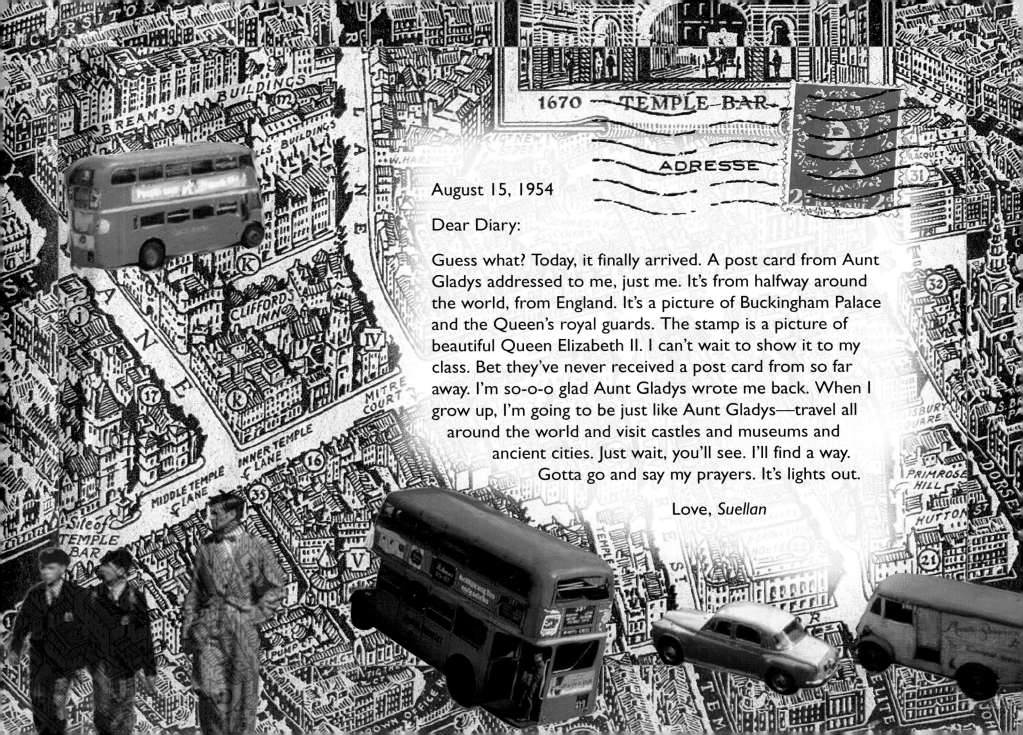

1670 TEMPLE BAR

ADRESSE

August 15, 1954

Dear Diary:

Guess what? Today, it finally arrived. A post card from Aunt Gladys addressed to me, just me. It's from halfway around the world, from England. It's a picture of Buckingham Palace and the Queen's royal guards. The stamp is a picture of beautiful Queen Elizabeth II. I can't wait to show it to my class. Bet they've never received a post card from so far away. I'm so-o-o glad Aunt Gladys wrote me back. When I grow up, I'm going to be just like Aunt Gladys—travel all around the world and visit castles and museums and ancient cities. Just wait, you'll see. I'll find a way. Gotta go and say my prayers. It's lights out.

Love, *Suellan*

Dear Aunt Gladys:

How are you? I am fine. I love the post card from Buckingham
Palace. Did you have tea and scones with the Queen? Mom said
scones taste kinda like Grandma Weaver's home-made biscuits.
There's not much happening here. Brownie still chases lizards &
snakes. School is ok. I'm in the 4th grade now. My favorite
subject is history. I'm a really good drawer and the *best* tether
ball player. I'm changing my name to Susan, cause my teacher
calls me "Swellan." Do you think Susan suits me? Mom says it
fits me fine. I have to go now & practice cello. Please write back!

  Love,

  Susan

P.S. Have you been to Mexico?
We buy tamales & fruit there.

Oct 22, 1954

Dear Diary:

Today mom taught me how to play Aunt Gladys' favorite song, "Somewhere over the rainbow." And, she told us stories about Grandma Grace, Aunt Gladys and Aunt Celia when they were little girls. I thought they were born rich, but they weren't. In fact, their family was really poor. Their mother died when they were very young and their father, my great grandfather, worked in the mines. But then he lost his leg in an accident and couldn't work the mines anymore. The only job he could get was to sweep the village streets and take care of the local cemetery. But they *always* had food…they had a great big cabbage patch in their back yard. Mom said he married a fun gal—she played the pump organ. Great-Grandpa played the violin. I asked Mom how a girl from a poor family could get rich enough to travel all over the world. Mom said, Aunt Gladys was a hard worker—a school teacher for many years. And, Mom said she was born a dreamer… always imagining herself in some exotic place, far away…. Whenever anyone would ask her how she planned to get there, she would inform them "Where there's a will, there's a way." And, Mom said, Aunt Gladys *always* found a way. Tonight I'm going to sleep with the post card on my heart and imagine it is a magic carpet that will fly me over the mountains and across the seas to England. Good night. Sleep tight. Don't let the bedbugs bite….

Love, *Susan*

July, 1955

Dear Susan:

Everything in Switzerland is beautiful—the alps, the villages, the cows, the bells, the flowers...we went by train to the Jungfrau yesterday—13,650 ft...many glaciers. I hope one day you too can see this great, big wonder-full world. Glad you are a good student and artist. Keep practicing. Susan means graceful lily. It's a perfect name for you.

Love, *Aunt Glad*

P.S. I've been to Mexico, but not Nogales.

Placing the post card over her heart, Susan again dreamed…

Soaring through space, the post card carried her to all the faraway places Aunt Gladys visited....

Over the years, the postcards and photos continued to arrive from the far away places Aunt Gladys explored…

Susan would study them carefully, read the messages again and again... and dream of being in Hong Kong…or Paris…or Oslo…or Rome….

Dear Susan:

Japan (Nippon) is a fascinating country.
The larger cities, Tokyo, Kyoto and
Yokohama, have their old sections but the
new sections are very much westernized.
Everyone in a hurry. Lots of new
construction. I'm having a wonderful
time in these strange places with our fun
travel group. Having trouble sitting on
floor and eating with chop sticks. Back &
legs ache, lips full of splinters. Hai!
Tomorrow we fly to Hong Kong.

      Love,

         Aunt Glad

Dear Susan,

This is one of the most popular Buddhas on the tourist circuit—70% solid gold. But, there are Buddhas and Buddhist temples everywhere. Thailand, formerly Siam, is the one country in this hot spot area of "Reds" that does not seem concerned about Communism. There is no great wealth nor is anyone hungry. They are peace loving, happy people.

Love,

Aunt Glad

April 20, 1965

Dear Susan:

After a month of travel, I am still enjoying this "Trip of a Lifetime." Arrived here last evening and visited the beautiful Taj at sunrise this a.m. A place I have always dreamed* of seeing. We will see it again this evening at sunset when the colors reflected in the pure white marble are magnificent. It is truly a work of art. Do you still draw?

Love, *Glad*

*P. S. Remember, dreams do
come true!

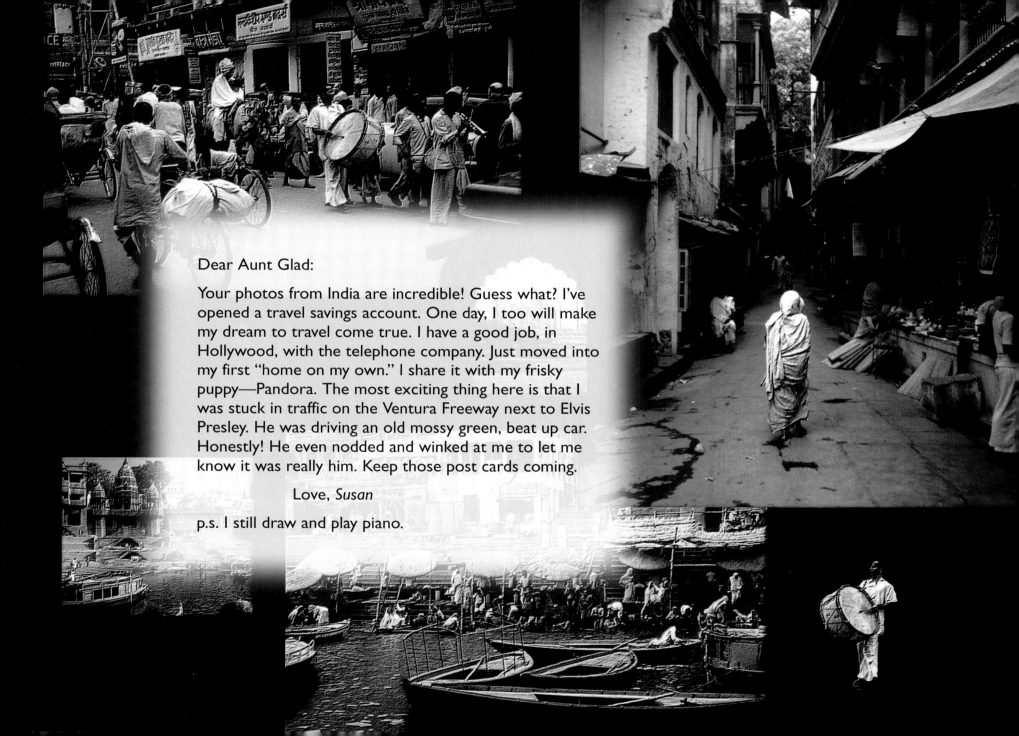

Dear Aunt Glad:

Your photos from India are incredible! Guess what? I've opened a travel savings account. One day, I too will make my dream to travel come true. I have a good job, in Hollywood, with the telephone company. Just moved into my first "home on my own." I share it with my frisky puppy—Pandora. The most exciting thing here is that I was stuck in traffic on the Ventura Freeway next to Elvis Presley. He was driving an old mossy green, beat up car. Honestly! He even nodded and winked at me to let me know it was really him. Keep those post cards coming.

Love, *Susan*

p.s. I still draw and play piano.

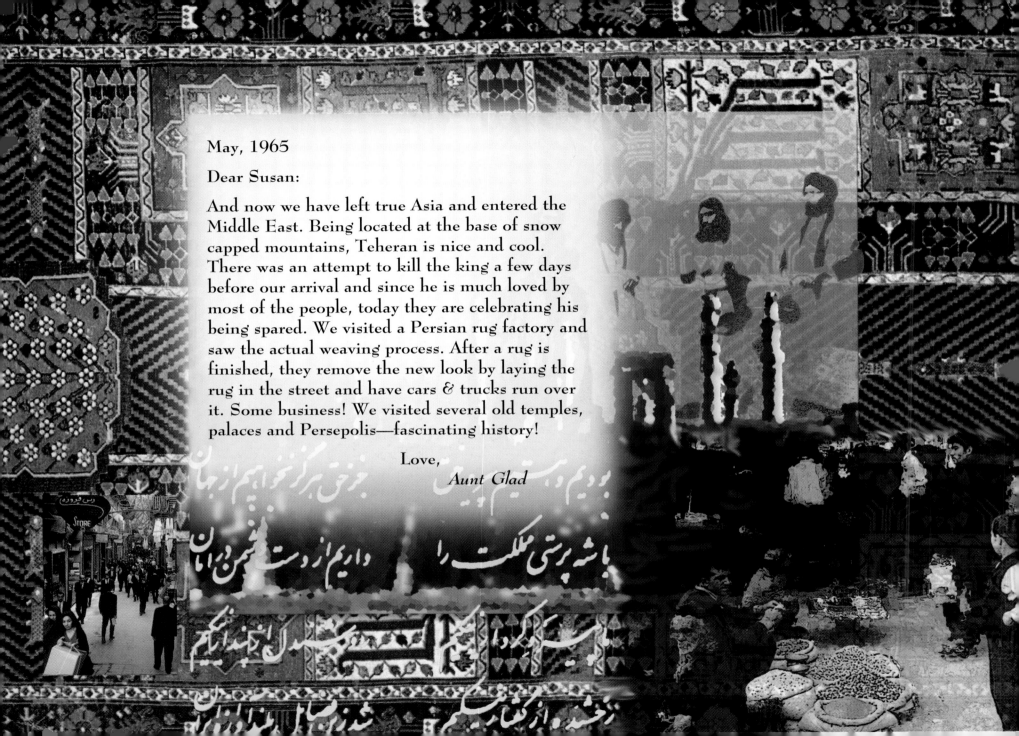

May, 1965

Dear Susan:

And now we have left true Asia and entered the Middle East. Being located at the base of snow capped mountains, Teheran is nice and cool. There was an attempt to kill the king a few days before our arrival and since he is much loved by most of the people, today they are celebrating his being spared. We visited a Persian rug factory and saw the actual weaving process. After a rug is finished, they remove the new look by laying the rug in the street and have cars & trucks run over it. Some business! We visited several old temples, palaces and Persepolis—fascinating history!

Love,
Aunt Glad

Dear Susan:

Greetings from the City of a thousand and one nights, Ali Baba and his 40 thieves, Aladdin and his magic lamp, the Flying Carpet and tourist traps everywhere. Baghdad is on the Tigris River—of much fame in history and my hotel room "looked" out upon it. Saw the Hanging Gardens (one of the ancient 7 wonders of the world) in the ruins of old Babylon on the Euphrates.

Love,
Glad

WELCOME TO BAGHDAD

Dear Susan:

Our hotel is on the top of the Mount of Olives. From my window I see a panoramic view of the entire city of Jerusalem— another dream come true. The old city is magical with its covered bazaar, where you can buy anything from a pin to a camel. We drove to Bethlehem, then on to Bethany where we visited the home of Lazarus and took an over-night trip to Petra, 250 miles south of Jerusalem and on the way stopped at Jericho, the oldest (7,000 years) continuously inhabited city in the world. Remember the song "...the walls came tumbling down."

Love, *Glad*

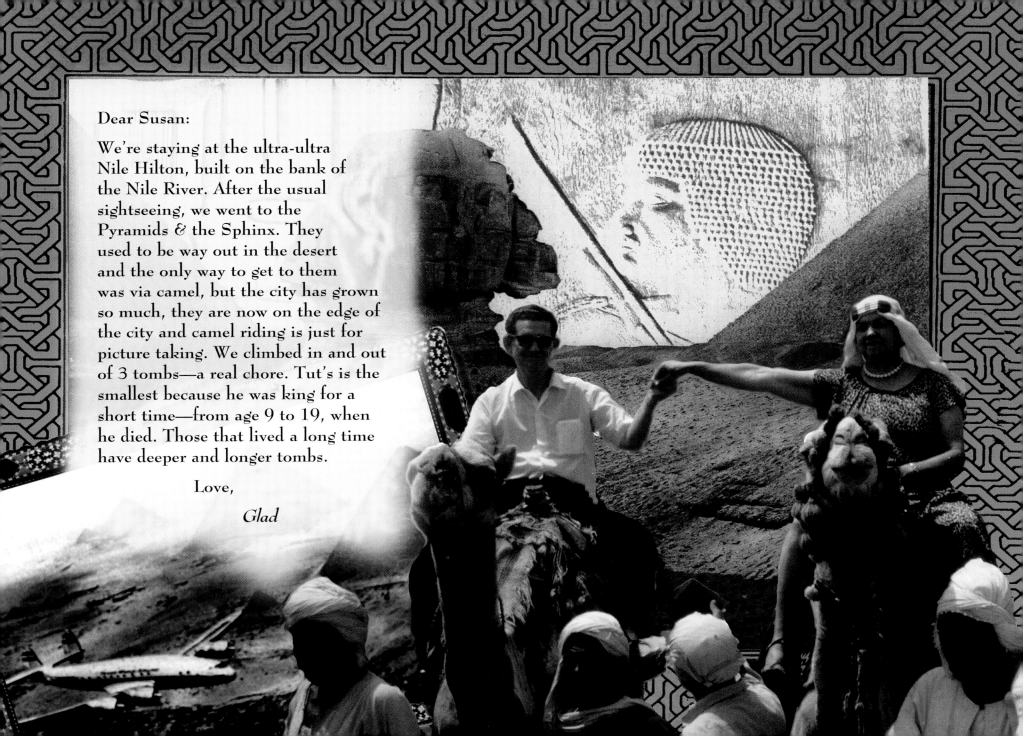

Dear Susan:

We're staying at the ultra-ultra Nile Hilton, built on the bank of the Nile River. After the usual sightseeing, we went to the Pyramids & the Sphinx. They used to be way out in the desert and the only way to get to them was via camel, but the city has grown so much, they are now on the edge of the city and camel riding is just for picture taking. We climbed in and out of 3 tombs—a real chore. Tut's is the smallest because he was king for a short time—from age 9 to 19, when he died. Those that lived a long time have deeper and longer tombs.

Love,

Glad

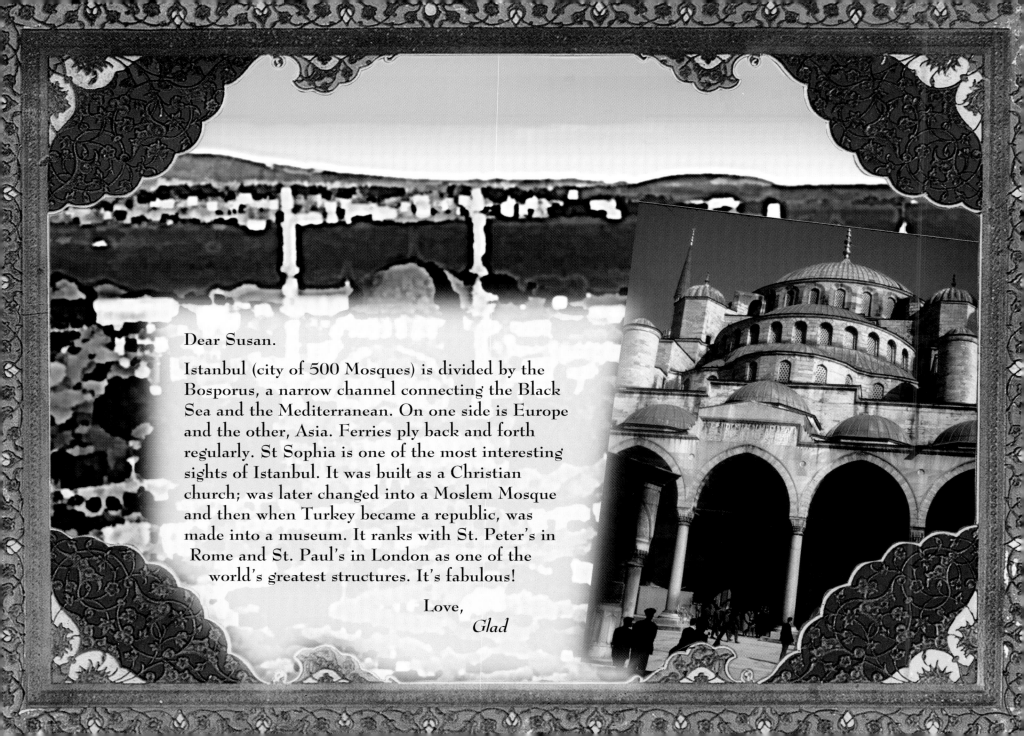

Dear Susan.

Istanbul (city of 500 Mosques) is divided by the Bosporus, a narrow channel connecting the Black Sea and the Mediterranean. On one side is Europe and the other, Asia. Ferries ply back and forth regularly. St Sophia is one of the most interesting sights of Istanbul. It was built as a Christian church; was later changed into a Moslem Mosque and then when Turkey became a republic, was made into a museum. It ranks with St. Peter's in Rome and St. Paul's in London as one of the world's greatest structures. It's fabulous!

Love,

Glad

Dear Susan,

The Athens Hilton is great! We watched dancers dance the famous "kalamatianos," the Greek national dance. One dancer leads waving a handkerchief as he steps and leaps (scherza) and he throws the handkerchief to another dancer when he grows tired. Athens is a wonderful city. So much to see. This is really the trip of a lifetime. "Ka-la" which means really good.

Love, *Glad*

P.S. Keep dreaming—and saving!

Dear Susan:

Dubrovnik is a beautiful feudal city built on a narrow strip of land between the mountains and the Adriatic Sea—behind the Iron Curtain. Everything is owned and operated by The State and whatever The State decrees, the people do... Our reservations at the Excelsior Hotel (the only first class hotel in the city) were cancelled because an important "Communist Party" conference is being held there. We are staying at a 2nd class hotel, the Petha. It's satisfactory. I have a good view of the Adriatic and cruise ships stopping to take on fresh supplies. We enjoyed a scenic tour along the coast to a village called St Stephan where we had an excellent lunch with fine native wine. We leave tomorrow for London. From England, It's out to sea on the Queen Elizabeth with our next stop being New York and home.

Love,

Glad

Sept, 1967

Dear Aunt Glad:

Tried calling you with my exciting news, but you're somewhere... "over the rainbow." At last, I have saved enough to travel and see this great, big, wonder-full world. I quit my job, sold my belongings, found a good home (heaven!) for Pandora. My bags are packed. First stop is London town, on my around the world in one year trip. I'll think of you as I sip tea and nibble scones and I promise to send post cards from all the places I visit.

Love,

Susan

P.S. Thank you for everything!

Library of Congress
Cataloging-in-Publication Data

Joyce, Susan, 1945-
  Post Card passages / written by Susan Joyce :
illustrated by Doug DuBosque.
  Summary: Great-aunt Gladys sends postcards
from her travels to young Susan, who is
inspired to work and dream and save until she
too can travel around the world.
  ISBN 0-939217-27-9 : $13.95
  [1. Travel--Fiction. 2. Postcards--Fiction. 3.
Great-aunts--Fiction.] I. DuBosque, D. C., ill.
II. Title.
PZ7.J856Po   1994
[E]--dc20   94-2949 CIP

Text copyright ©1994 Susan Joyce.
Illustrations copyright ©1994 Doug DuBosque

ISBN 0-939217-27-9 (hc)

        2   4   5   3   1

Published by Peel Productions
PO Box 185, Molalla, Oregon USA 97038-0185

Printed and bound in Hong Kong